This book
belongs to

. . . .

First published in 2017 by Miles Kelly Publishing Ltd
Harding's Barn, Bardfield End Green, Thaxted, Essex, CM6 3PX, UK

2 4 6 8 10 9 7 5 3 1

Publishing Director Belinda Gallagher
Creative Director Jo Cowan
Editorial Director Rosie Neave
Senior Editor Fran Bromage
Senior Designer Rob Hale
Image Manager Liberty Newton
Production Elizabeth Collins, Caroline Kelly
Reprographics Stephan Davis, Jennifer Cozens
Assets Lorraine King

ISBN 978-1-78617-239-6

Printed in China

British Library Cataloguing-in-Publication Data
A catalogue record for this book is available from the British Library

Made with paper from a sustainable forest

www.mileskelly.net

Read Me a Story

Compiled by
Catherine Veitch

Miles Kelly

Contents

TASTY TALES
6-67

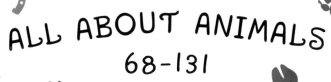

ALL ABOUT ANIMALS
68-131

TOWERING GIANTS AND TINY PEOPLE
132-197

AMAZING ADVENTURES

198-255

STRANGE SPELLS

256-321

MAGICAL LANDS

322-383

About the Artists

384

TASTY TALES

The Gingerbread Man 8

The King's Magic Drum 17

Hansel and Gretel 27

The Elephant's Child 40

The Three Wishes 47

Goldilocks and the Three Bears 56

The Gingerbread Man

One day a woman was making some gingerbread biscuits. With a little leftover dough, she made a gingerbread man. She used two shiny black

The Gingerbread Man

currants for eyes and chocolate drops for buttons.

Then the gingerbread man was ready to bake in the oven. He looked like a cheeky fellow. The woman had better keep an eye on him!

Soon the biscuits were cooked. The woman took the tray out of the oven, but with a hop, skip and a jump, the gingerbread man headed off across the kitchen.

The woman shouted to her husband, and together they ran after the little gingerbread man. But the gingerbread man shot out of the kitchen door, saying,

The Gingerbread Man

"Run, run, as
fast as you can! You
can't catch me, I'm the
gingerbread man!"

Outside, the gingerbread man
leapt over a sleeping cat. The
husband shouted, "Fluffy! Stop

the gingerbread man!" So the
cat jumped up, and the woman
and the man, and the cat ran
after the gingerbread man.

They followed him down to

The Gingerbread Man

the garden, where their dog was chasing its tail. And the husband shouted, "Spot, help us! Stop the gingerbread man."

So the woman and the man, the cat and the dog all ran after the gingerbread man.

But the gingerbread man sang, "Run, run, as fast as you can! You can't catch me, I'm the gingerbread man!"

The gingerbread man climbed over a little stone wall and came to a wide river. "I can't cross this river," he cried. But a sly fox heard him and said, "Little man, jump on my back and I'll give you a lift across."

So the gingerbread man

climbed onto the fox's back and the fox started swimming. Soon, water was splashing up the fox's back, so the gingerbread man climbed onto the fox's head.

The fox was hungry and the gingerbread man smelled delicious. The cunning fox sank down into the water a bit more, and the gingerbread man had to climb onto the fox's nose so he didn't get wet.

TASTY TALES

Once the gingerbread man had settled onto the fox's nose, the fox tossed his head. The gingerbread man flew into the air as the fox opened his mouth.

When the fox reached the other side of the river, all that was left of the gingerbread man were a few tasty crumbs.

The King's Magic Drum

A long time ago, in a land far away, there lived a king. The king had a magic drum that gave him food every time he beat it. But there was a problem with the King's drum. If he stepped on a stick when he was carrying his magic drum, all the food would go bad.

Every few months the King invited all of his people to his castle for a feast. Even the animals were invited. The King banged his magic drum and everyone enjoyed eating food of every description and flavour.

One day, a tortoise and the

king had an argument. The King felt bad about the fight, so to make up for it, he agreed to give the tortoise anything that he wanted.

The tortoise asked for the king's magic drum. Now the King was a man of his word, so he handed it over.

The tortoise hurried home. "I am rich," he told his wife. "Whenever I want food, all I

have to do is beat this drum."
The tortoise's wife and children
were hungry so they asked for
food at once. The tortoise beat
the drum and sure enough, food
magically appeared for them all.

The King's Magic Drum

Over time the tortoise became lazy and stopped working. His family grew fat and had more food than they could possibly eat.

One day when the tortoise was walking home carrying his drum, he stepped on a stick. When he got home all the food in his house had gone bad.

The tortoise didn't see why he should be the only one to eat

bad food. So he invited all his friends over, and gave them the bad food too.

After this, the tortoise felt fed up with the drum, so he gave it back to the king. The King felt sorry for the tortoise, so he gave him a magic tree, which would also give him food.

"But," said the King, "you can only get food from the tree once a day." The tortoise thanked the king for his kindness and went home to his family.

Once a day the tortoise went to the magic tree to get food, but one of his sons was greedy and wanted more. His father wouldn't tell him where the magic tree was, so the son followed his father to the magic

tree. Then when his father had
left, the son asked the
tree for more food.

The next day when the tortoise
went to get more food, he
couldn't find the magic tree.

Instead there was a prickly bush in its place. The tortoise guessed that someone had asked the tree for more food.

The tortoise brought his family to the prickly bush. He told them that from that day on the leaves from the prickly bush were all the food they had.

So the tortoise family made their home under the prickly bush. From this day on you will always find tortoises living under prickly bushes, because they have nowhere else to go for their food.

Hansel and Gretel

A long time ago a poor woodcutter lived with his two children, Hansel and Gretel, in a cottage by a forest. The woodcutter's wife had died and he had married again. His new wife was mean and didn't like Hansel and Gretel.

One day the poor woodcutter said to his wife, "How are we to feed our children?" And his wife said, "We can't. Tomorrow you must take them into the forest and leave them there."

The woodcutter didn't want to leave his children, but his wife whispered mean words in his

ear all night until he agreed.
They didn't know that Hansel
and Gretel could hear them.
Gretel was afraid, but Hansel
had an idea.

Later that night, Hansel crept
out of the house and picked up
as many little white stones as he
could fit in his pockets. Then he
went to bed.

In the morning, the
woodcutter took the children

into the forest. Hansel dropped the white stones out of his pockets one by one, until they got to the middle of the forest.

Hansel and Gretel

There, the woodcutter lit a fire and told the children to rest.

The children soon fell asleep by the fire, and the woodcutter left them. When they woke up, it was night time. Gretel was frightened and cried, "How will we get out of the forest?"

But Hansel took her hand and pointed to the little white stones he had dropped on the way. The stones shone in the

moonlight so they were able to follow them all the way home. Their father was happy to see them, but their stepmother was angry they were back.

Soon the family's food ran out again, and the stepmother told the woodcutter to take the children away in the morning. Hansel told Gretel not to worry, but that night their stepmother locked the door. Hansel couldn't

get out to find any stones.

In the morning, their father gave the children some bread. Hansel saved his, and as they walked through the forest he dropped crumbs on the ground.

They went deeper into the forest this time. As before, the woodcutter lit a fire and told the children to stay and rest by it.

When Hansel and Gretel woke up, it was dark again.

Hansel looked for the crumbs to show them the way home, but the birds had eaten them all.

The children started walking. After a long time, they spotted a little house made of bread, cakes and sweets. The hungry children broke off bits to eat. It was so tasty!

Suddenly, an old woman appeared and invited the children inside. She showed

them to a bedroom where they could rest, and the children went to sleep, full and happy.

But the old woman was really a mean witch who planned to eat them. The next morning, she grabbed Hansel and pushed him into a cage. Then she made Gretel cook for her brother. "Feed him lots of food, and I'll eat him when he's fat!" she said.

Every morning the witch told

Hansel to stick out his finger so she could check he was growing fat. The witch couldn't see very well, so Hansel stuck out a thin stick, so she would think he wasn't getting fat at all.

After a few weeks the witch decided to eat Hansel anyway. She asked Gretel to climb into her big oven to light it. But Gretel said, "I don't know how to light it. Can you show me?"

As soon as the old woman
climbed into the oven, Gretel
slammed the oven door shut,

trapping the witch inside.

Gretel let Hansel out of the cage and the two children ran out of the house, into the forest. Eventually they found their way home and their father was delighted to see them. Their stepmother had left, so they lived happily ever after.

The Elephant's Child

A long time ago the Elephant had no trunk. Instead he had a big, fat nose as large as a boot, which he wriggled from side to side.

The Elephant's Child

There was one little Elephant's Child who always asked lots of questions. The world seemed strange to him. He asked his hairy uncle, the Baboon, why melons tasted just so. And he asked his tall, tall uncle, the Giraffe, what made his skin spotty.

One morning, the Elephant's Child asked, "What does the Crocodile have for dinner?"

No one could answer the Elephant's Child's question so he set off on his own to find out.

He reached a long, green river, and trod on what he thought was a large log, but it was actually a Crocodile.

The Elephant's Child

"Excuse me," the Elephant's Child said to the log. "Have you seen a Crocodile around here?"

"Why?" said the Crocodile.

"I want to know what a Crocodile eats for dinner," said the Elephant's Child.

"I am a Crocodile," said the Crocodile. And with that, he grabbed hold of the Elephant's Child's nose and pulled him towards the river.

TASTY TALES

"I'll eat Elephant's Child for my dinner today!" said the Crocodile between his teeth.

The Elephant's Child tried to pull away, but as the Crocodile pulled one way, the Elephant's Child pulled the other, and the Elephant's Child's nose grew longer.

A Snake saw the

The Elephant's Child

Elephant's Child was in trouble, so he wrapped himself around the Elephant's Child's legs. And the Snake pulled and pulled too.

Together, the Elephant's Child and the Snake were too strong for the Crocodile and... plop!

Finally the Crocodile let go of the Elephant's Child's nose.

But the Elephant's Child's nose never went back to its old shape. And that is why elephants today have very, very long noses.

The Three Wishes

Long ago there was a poor farmer who worked very hard. He lived with his wife in a little cottage.

Every day the farmer worked

long hours in the fields. One day he had been planting rows and rows of potatoes. He was just covering the last potato with soil when he heard a little voice say, "Please don't put soil over me."

The farmer wondered where the voice came from. He couldn't see anyone, so he carried on shovelling soil. But then he heard the voice again and it was a little louder this time.

The Three Wishes

"Please don't cover me up." The farmer looked at the potato and saw it had changed into a tiny fairy. The farmer didn't think he should try to plant the pretty fairy so he stopped shovelling soil.

TASTY TALES

"Thank you for not burying me," said the little fairy. And to show how pleased she was, she gave the farmer three wishes. "But be careful," she said, "wishes don't always give you what you really want."

The farmer picked up his tools and set off home. It was a long way and the farmer was tired when he got back. He settled into his chair by the fire and told his wife all about the fairy and the three wishes. But the farmer had forgotten all about the fairy's warning. His wife just laughed at him for believing in fairies.

"What's for dinner?" he asked, to change the subject.

"Soup. The same as every day," said his wife.

"Ah," groaned the farmer. "I wish I had some chicken!"

TASTY TALES

No sooner had the farmer wished this, when... clatter, clatter, rustle, rustle! The finest chicken he could ever have wished for, fell down the chimney. But his wife wasn't happy.

"You fool! Why didn't you wish for gold?" she moaned. "Uh, I wish that chicken was on your head!" And in a flash the chicken plopped on the farmer's head. The farmer's wife had made a wish by mistake!

The farmer tried to pull the chicken off his head. Then his wife tried. Then they both pulled, and pulled, and pulled. But the chicken wouldn't come off the farmer's head.

"What shall we do?" said

the farmer in a panic. They only had one wish left, but they both knew that the farmer couldn't live with a chicken on his head.

So together they both said, "We wish the chicken was off the farmer's head." Immediately the chicken dropped off the farmer's head and landed with a thump on a plate.

The farmer and his wife sighed sadly. They had used up

The Three Wishes

all their wishes without meaning to, but they did enjoy a lovely meal of roast chicken that night.

Goldilocks and the Three Bears

Once upon a time there were three bears who lived in a small house in the woods. There was Papa Bear, Mama Bear and Baby Bear. In another cottage nearby there lived a little girl called Goldilocks and her family.

One morning the three bears went for a walk in the woods, while their porridge was cooling. That morning Goldilocks was also walking in the woods – although her mother had told her never to go walking alone.

Goldilocks found the house belonging to the three bears and peeped through the window.

There didn't seem to be anyone home, so she opened the door.

Inside was a table laid with three bowls of steaming hot porridge. There was a big bowl, a medium-sized bowl and a little bowl. The porridge smelled sweet and delicious.

If Goldilocks had been polite, she would have waited until the bears came home and asked them for some porridge. But

59

instead, she walked into the house and helped herself.

First, Goldilocks tasted the porridge from the big bowl, but it was too hot. Then she tasted the porridge in the medium bowl, which was too cold. Finally she tasted the porridge from the little bowl, which tasted just right. Goldilocks ate it all up.

After that, Goldilocks wanted a rest, and tried sitting in a big chair, but it was much too hard. Then she tried the medium-sized chair, but that was too soft. Next Goldilocks tried the little chair, which was just right. But as she was getting comfy, there was a loud crack and the chair broke into pieces.

Goldilocks thought she would have a look upstairs. She found three beds and lay down on the biggest one. It was far too hard.

Then she tried the middle bed, which was too soft. Next she lay on the smallest bed – it was perfect! Goldilocks soon fell asleep.

Goldilocks and the Three Bears

Not long after this,
the bears arrived home.
Papa Bear looked at his
bowl and growled,
   "Somebody has been
eating my porridge!"
Mama Bear looked at
her bowl and grumbled,
"Somebody has been eating
my porridge!" Then Baby
Bear looked at his bowl and
cried, "Somebody has been

63

eating my porridge, and look, they've eaten it all up!"

Next the bears saw their chairs had been moved around. Papa Bear growled, "Somebody has been sitting in my chair!"

Mama Bear looked at her chair and grumbled, "Somebody has been sitting in my chair!"

Then Baby Bear looked at his chair and began to cry. He said, "Somebody has been sitting in

my chair and has broken it!"

Then the bears went upstairs to look at their beds. Papa Bear growled in his big, gruff voice, "Somebody has been lying in my bed!" And Mama Bear looked at her middle-sized bed and grumbled, "Somebody has been lying in my bed!"

Then Baby Bear looked at his little bed and whispered, "Look! Somebody has been lying in my

bed and they're still here!"
Suddenly Goldilocks woke up.
She saw the three cross bears
staring at her.

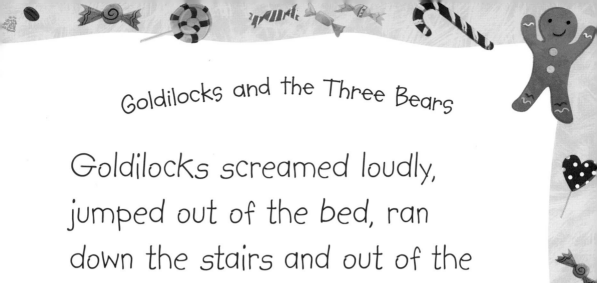

Goldilocks screamed loudly, jumped out of the bed, ran down the stairs and out of the door as fast as she could. And the three bears never saw Goldilocks again.

ALL ABOUT ANIMALS

The Three Little Pigs 70

How the Rhinoceros Got His Skin 80

Puss in Boots 88

Moray Monkey Gets Lost 98

The Lion and the Mouse 108

Raggedy Ann and the Kittens 114

The Hare and the Tortoise 124

The Three Little Pigs

Once upon a time, there were three little pigs. One day it was time for them to leave home. Each little pig wanted to build their own house.

The Three Little Pigs

The first little pig met a man with some straw. He said to the man, "Please can I have some of your straw to build a house?"

So the man gave the first little pig some

straw. The little pig built a super straw house, but it was not long finished when a big, bad wolf knocked at his door.

"Little pig, little pig, let me come in," said the wolf.

"Not by the hair on my chinny, chin, chin!" squeaked the first little pig.

"Then I'll huff, and I'll puff, and I'll blow your house down!" shouted the wolf. And he huffed and he puffed, and he blew the straw house down. The first little pig ran away.

The second little pig had met a man with some sticks. He said to the man, "Please can I have some sticks to build a house?"

So the man gave him some sticks, and the

little pig built a spectacular stick house. No sooner was the house finished than the big, bad wolf came knocking at his door.

"Little pig, little pig, let me come in," growled the wolf.

"Not by the hair on my chinny, chin, chin!" squeaked the second little pig.

"Then I'll huff, and I'll puff, and I'll blow your house down!" shouted the wolf. And he huffed and he puffed, and he blew the stick house down. The little pig ran off to find his brother.

75

The third little pig met a man with some bricks. She said to the man, "Please can I have some bricks to build a house?" So the man gave the third little

76

pig some bricks. Just as she had finished her brilliant brick house, her brothers arrived and told her about the wolf. The pigs hid inside the brick house and locked the door. At once, the big, bad wolf came knocking.

"Little pig, little pig, let me come in," roared the wolf.

"Not by the hair on my chinny, chin, chin!" squeaked the third little pig.

"Then I'll huff, and I'll puff, and I'll blow your house down!" shouted the wolf. And he huffed and he puffed, but not a single brick moved. The three little pigs looked out of the window and laughed.

At that, the angry wolf climbed onto the roof and got into the chimney. The third little pig guessed what he was doing and quickly put a big pot of water on the fire. When the wolf came down the chimney, he fell straight into the boiling water.

The wolf ran howling out of the house, and the three little pigs lived happily ever after in the little brick house.

How the Rhinoceros Got His Skin

A long time ago a man called
a Parsee lived on an island.
One day the Parsee made an
enormous cake on the beach.
He mixed in water, flour, sugar,

currants and plums, and baked it until it was brown all over and smelled delicious.

Just as the Parsee was about to eat his cake a Rhinoceros arrived. The Parsee was scared of the Rhinoceros so he climbed up a tree.

The Rhinoceros had a horn on his nose, two beady eyes and his skin fitted him quite tightly. There were no wrinkles in it

anywhere. The Rhinoceros had
no manners so he gobbled up
the Parsee's cake. Then he went
away, happily waving his tail.

The Parsee came down from
the tree and sang, "If you
eat a cake, that the
Parsee man has
baked, you're
making a
very big
mistake!"

Five weeks later the Rhinoceros found out the mistake he had made. It was such a hot summer, that everyone took off their clothes to swim in the sea. In those days, the Rhinoceros had skin buttoned underneath with three buttons. The Rhinoceros unbuttoned his skin and left it on the beach to go in the sea.

A little later, the Parsee came down to the beach and saw the skin, and he smiled a very big smile. Then he danced three times round the skin and clapped his hands.

The Parsee went home and filled a hat with cake crumbs. Then he came back to the beach and scattered the crumbs all over the Rhinoceros's skin. He shook and scrubbed and rubbed the skin all over with the dry, stale, tickly cake crumbs. Then the Parsee climbed a tree and waited for the Rhinoceros.

Soon the Rhinoceros came out of the sea. He buttoned up the three buttons and his skin started tickling him. He wanted to scratch, but it only seemed to make the itching worse. So the Rhinoceros lay down on the sand and rolled and rolled around. But the cake crumbs just tickled him more and more.

Then he ran to a palm tree and rubbed and rubbed. The Rhinoceros rubbed so much and so hard, he rubbed his skin into lots of loose folds. And his buttons popped right off.

The Rhinoceros went home

very angry and horribly itchy. And from that day on, every rhinoceros has wrinkly skin and a very bad temper.

Puss in Boots

Once upon a time there was
a miller who had three sons.
When the miller died he left his
mill to his eldest son, a donkey
to his middle son and to his

youngest son, he left his cat called Puss.

"What am I to do with a cat?" said the youngest son. Imagine his surprise when Puss replied, "Give me a bag and some boots, and I'll show you what I can do for you." So the youngest son fetched Puss a bag and some boots.

Puss caught a rabbit in his bag and took it to the king. He

said to the King, "This rabbit is from the Marquis of Carabas." (This was a name that Puss had made up for the youngest son.) The King was very pleased.

The next day Puss caught a large bird in his bag. He took the bird to the King, again saying it was from the Marquis of Carabas. For the next few months Puss gave the king many gifts from the pretend Marquis of Carabas.

One day Puss heard that the king and his beautiful daughter were to ride along the river. So he told the miller's youngest son

that he needed to swim in the river at that time.

When the king and his daughter rode past, Puss leapt in front of the king's carriage. "Help!" Puss cried. "Quick! The Marquis is drowning!"

The king's men pulled the youngest son out of the river and fetched him some dry clothes. They thought he really was the Marquis of Carabas, so the king asked him to sit in the carriage with him. The princess thought he was very handsome.

Puss ran on ahead of the carriage. He met some farm workers collecting hay in a field and said, "When the king asks, say this land belongs to the Marquis of Carabas." So when the king passed, this is what they did.

Puss went on ahead and met some farmers collecting corn. He said, "Tell the king this corn belongs to the Marquis of Carabas." Sure enough, a little later this is what they said.

The King thought the Marquis was a very rich and

generous man. 'This man would make a good husband for my daughter,' he thought to himself.

Finally Puss came to a castle where a cruel giant lived. Puss had heard that the giant could change into any animal he wanted and decided to trick him.

Clever Puss said to the giant, "I've heard that you can do magic. If it is true, then change yourself into a mouse!"

The giant enjoyed showing off, so he laughed at Puss and quickly changed himself into a tiny mouse. At once, Puss pounced on the mouse and ate it up.

That was the end of the giant!

"Welcome to the Marquis of Carabas's castle," Puss said, as the carriage arrived. The King was so impressed he offered the miller's son his daughter's hand in marriage, and they lived happily ever after.

Moray Monkey Gets Lost

Moray Monkey had always been told by his mummy and daddy never to play beyond the edge of the jungle. But there was a big log near the edge that Moray Monkey had always wanted to investigate.

One day, as he was playing hide-and-seek with his friends, he thought the log lying on its side would make the best hiding place. So Moray Monkey crawled inside it.

It was dark inside the log and Moray couldn't see or hear anything. After a while, when his friends hadn't found him, Moray crawled out. He had stayed inside the log much longer than he thought.

"Maddie! Mia!" Moray called, wandering around. But there was no answer. His friends had gone, and Moray realized he'd strayed quite far from home and didn't know the way back again.

It was hot out in the open, so Moray headed

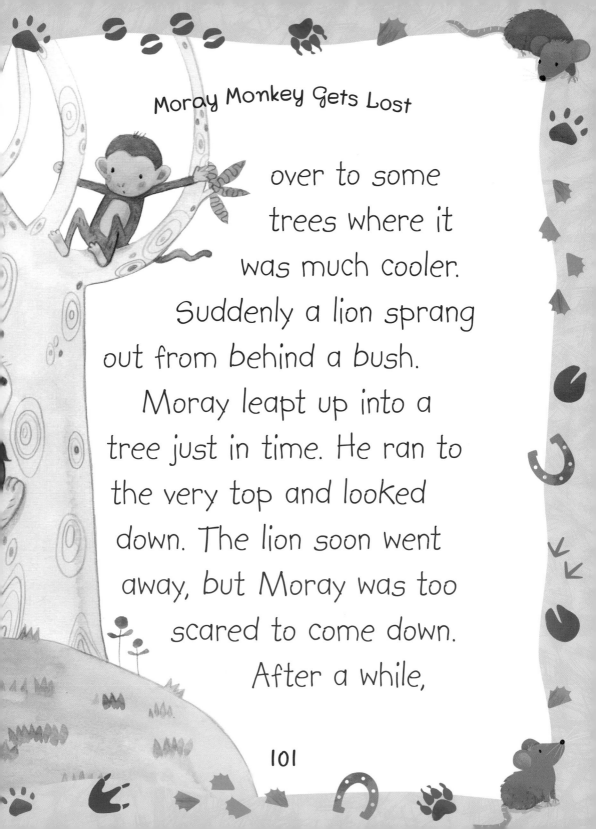

Moray Monkey Gets Lost

over to some trees where it was much cooler. Suddenly a lion sprang out from behind a bush. Moray leapt up into a tree just in time. He ran to the very top and looked down. The lion soon went away, but Moray was too scared to come down. After a while,

Moray heard a munching noise. Someone was pulling the leaves off the tree. Moray was scared they would pull him off too, so he held on tight. A soft, brown nose nuzzled into Moray and a black prickly tongue licked him.

"Please don't eat me!" cried Moray. "I won't eat you," said Gerry Giraffe. "You poor little thing. What are you doing up this tree all alone?"

Moray Monkey Gets Lost

Moray told Gerry his story. "Don't be scared. Slide down my neck," said Gerry. So Moray let go of the tree. He slid down Gerry's long neck, along his body, down his tail and onto the ground. Gerry showed him the way back into the jungle, and Moray went on his way.

But it wasn't long before Moray was lost again and he came to a wide, rushing river.

ALL ABOUT ANIMALS

"How can I get across this river?" Moray cried. Just then a big, grey head bobbed up from under the water.

"Can I help you?" said Hattie Hippo. And Moray told Hattie his story. "My friends and I will help you cross the water," said Hattie. "Jump on our heads and bounce

across," she smiled. So Moray did just that and was across the wide river in no time.

Moray looked up at the sky and saw it was nearly dark. Just then, a large stork flew overhead.

The stork thought it was strange that a young monkey was so far from home. So it flew down to see if it could help.

Moray told Saburo Stork his story. "We will see if we can spot your home from the air," said Saburo, grabbing Moray.

Up and up, she flew over the jungle. Then down and down she went, until they reached the ground with a bump.

Moray Monkey Gets Lost

Moray spotted his mummy and daddy and rushed into their arms. It was good to be home. He told them all about the kind animals who had helped him. "But," Moray said, "I'll listen to you from now on." And he never played as far away from home ever again.

The Lion
and the
Mouse

There was once a hungry lion looking for something to eat. He smelled a mouse and decided to follow it quietly through the long grass.

The Lion and the Mouse

"Rrrrroar!" the lion pounced on the mouse and caught it with his big paws.

"Please don't eat me!" begged the little mouse. "If you let me go, one day I may be able to help you."

The lion roared with laughter at the little mouse. As if she could help a great big lion! But he did think the mouse was very brave, so he let her go.

Not long after this the lion was hunting for food again. He smelled a rabbit and followed it through the grass. Suddenly a net made of strong rope fell on the lion. It was a trap left by hunters. The lion twisted and turned, but he couldn't break free of the ropes.

"Help!" he roared. But no one heard him. The lion was getting tired and had almost given up, when he heard a tiny voice.

"I told you that maybe one day I could help," said the little

mouse. The lion was pleased to
see his friend, but he didn't
know how the mouse could help.

"Leave this to me," said the
mouse. And she nibbled, gnawed
and chewed at the ropes. One

by one, she chewed through them all, until the lion was free.

"Thank you my dear little friend," said the lion.

"Sometimes even the smallest animal can be a big help," said the mouse.

"How right you are," replied the grateful lion.

Raggedy Ann and the Kittens

Raggedy Ann is Marcella's rag doll. She lives with Marcella, and Marcella's mummy and daddy.

One morning Marcella

dressed all her dolls and sat them on little red chairs around the doll's table in her playroom.

She put some turkey, a fried egg and an apple on the table for them. It wasn't real food, as Marcella was pretending, but she told her dolls to enjoy their meal while she was away. Then Marcella picked up Raggedy Ann and left the playroom.

When the door closed the tin

soldier winked at a tiny doll and handed her some pretend turkey. "Would you like some more?" he asked. "No, thank you," said the tiny doll. "I'm full up already."

Meanwhile, a Scottish doll called Uncle Clem played a song on the toy piano. He wasn't very good! Suddenly, they all heard a noise, so they quickly went back to the way Marcella had left them. For it was a secret that they could move and talk.

The noise was actually Fido, Marcella's dog. He pushed open the playroom door. "Where's

Raggedy Ann?," Fido asked. "I've got something to tell her." (Fido knew the dolls could talk.) The toys told him that Raggedy Ann had gone out with Marcella.

"There are some kittens in the shed outside, but it's dreadfully cold," said Fido.

"Oh, I wish Raggedy Ann was here!" cried the tiny French doll. "She would know what to do."

Finally, at the end of the day,

Raggedy Ann came back to the playroom and the dolls told her all about the kittens. Raggedy Ann said they should go out to the shed to see them.

They slipped through an open window of the playroom. Then they crawled through a hole in the shed's wall. Mamma Cat and her three kittens were in the corner of the shed.

The shed wasn't safe for the

little kittens, so Raggedy Ann told Mamma Cat to bring them into the house. "We'll help take them into the playroom!" said Raggedy Ann.

Raggedy Ann carried two of the kittens, and Mamma Cat carried one. Fido gave Mamma Cat and her kittens his bed, which had a soft blanket inside. Fido and the dolls were worried what Marcella would say when

she found the little kittens in the playroom, in the morning.

But next morning when Marcella ran into the playroom, the first thing she saw were the kittens. She was so excited, and shouted, "Mummy, Daddy, come and see what's in the playroom!"

Marcella's mummy and daddy said Marcella could keep Mamma Cat and her kittens in the playroom for the time being.

Marcella called the kittens Prince Charming, Cinderella and Princess Golden.

And that is how three kittens and their Mamma Cat came to live in Marcella's playroom.

The Hare and the Tortoise

A Hare was always boasting about how fast he was. He boasted so much that all the other animals were quite fed up listening to him.

The Hare and the Tortoise

One day, the Hare was out for a run when he spotted the Tortoise plodding along.

"You're so slow," the Hare laughed. The Tortoise stuck his head out of his shell and replied, "Let's have a race then, to see who's the fastest."

This made the Hare laugh more, because he thought he could beat the slow Tortoise any day. But he agreed to the race.

By the day of the race all of the animals had heard about it and were cheering at the start. The Fox was to start the race. "3, 2, 1, go!" shouted the Fox, and they were off.

Hare sprinted away, whipping up a cloud of dust under his big, back feet. He was out of sight in a moment. But the Tortoise's short, little legs didn't go very

fast and he crept
along at a slow,
but steady pace.
Part of the
way into the
race the Hare
passed a field
of big, yummy
lettuces. They
looked so tasty.
'I'm so far ahead of Tortoise,'
the Hare thought,

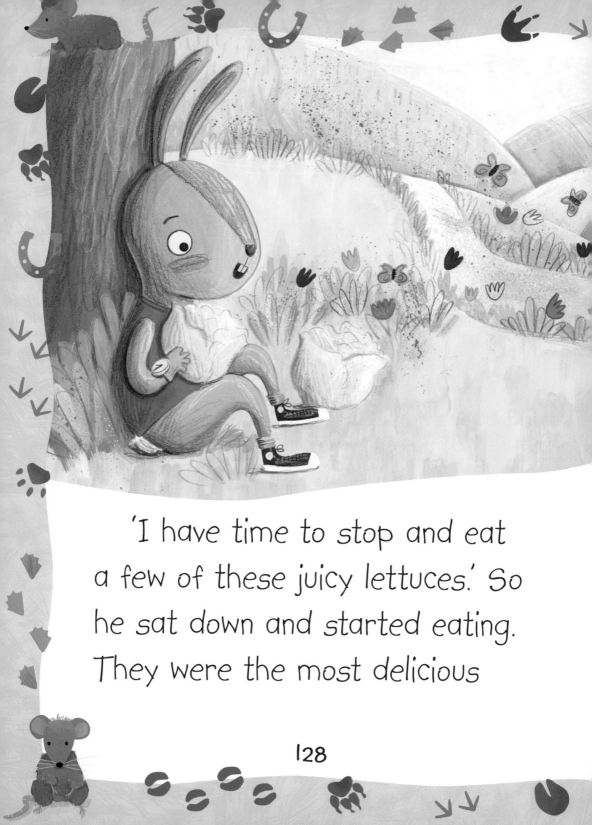

'I have time to stop and eat a few of these juicy lettuces.' So he sat down and started eating. They were the most delicious lettuces he'd ever tasted and soon the Hare had a full tummy.

It was a hot day, and he felt tired. 'I'm so far ahead of Tortoise,' the Hare thought to himself, 'I have plenty of time for a little sleep.'

So the Hare made some big, green leaves into a pillow and lay down in the field. He was soon fast asleep.

During this time the Tortoise

kept plodding along. He moved slowly, but he never stopped and he never gave up. After a while the Tortoise passed the field of lettuces where the Hare slept. And still the Hare slept on.

When the Tortoise got near to the finish line, the other animals cheered loudly. Their shouting woke up the Hare. He sprang up and shot across the field. He sped up to try to

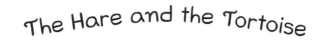

reach the finish line, but the Tortoise had just crossed it.

The Hare was too late! The Tortoise had won the race. "Slow and steady wins the race," said the Tortoise with a smile.

TOWERING GIANTS AND TINY PEOPLE

Jack and the Beanstalk 134

Tom Thumb 147

Snow White and the Seven Dwarfs 156

The Selfish Giant 169

Thumbelina 178

The Elves and the Shoemaker 188

133

Jack and the Beanstalk

Once upon a time a boy
called Jack lived with his
mother. They were very poor.
One day, Jack's mother told
him to take their cow to the

market to sell. Jack hadn't gone very far when he met an old man who offered to swap five beans for Jack's cow.

Jack wasn't so sure about the swap. But the old man said, "These beans are magic. Plant them at night and by morning they will have grown right up into the sky." So Jack took the five beans and gave the old man his cow in return.

Jack's mother was furious with Jack for swapping their cow for a few beans. "You're a fool and that man has tricked you," she said, and she threw the beans out of the window and

sent Jack straight to bed.

In the morning Jack looked outside and was amazed. The magic beans had grown into a huge beanstalk that went up and up, until it reached the sky! The little old man had been telling the truth.

Quickly Jack climbed the beanstalk. High up in the sky, sitting on a giant cloud was a big house. Standing outside the towering house was a giant woman who invited Jack in for breakfast and gave him some bread and cheese.

Jack had only eaten a little food, when he heard a loud thumping noise. The whole house started to shake.

"My husband is home," said the woman, "Quick, hide in here!" She pushed Jack into the oven. Jack peered out and saw the woman's enormous husband through the glass door of the oven. He was an immense giant!

"Fee fi fo fum, I smell the blood of an Englishman!" roared the giant, stomping around.

"Don't be silly dear. There's no one here," said his wife and told him to have a quick nap before breakfast.

When the giant was asleep, his wife told Jack to leave. Jack crept past the giant and stole a bag of gold, which was sitting at the snoring giant's feet.

Jack climbed down the beanstalk as fast as he could go and ran inside his house. He gave his mother the gold and said, "I was right about the beans. They are magical!"

Jack and his mother lived on the bag of gold for some time. But, when the money ran out

again, Jack climbed the
beanstalk to the house in
the sky.

Again, he met
the giant woman
outside and was

invited inside for breakfast. Jack had just taken one bite when he heard the thumping sound again.

"My husband is home!" cried the woman. This time Jack knew exactly where to hide and got into the oven.

Everything happened as before, with Jack hiding until the giant was asleep. This time as Jack crept past the dozing giant, he saw a golden hen sitting quietly at the giant's feet.

Jack picked up the golden hen, but it clucked loudly as Jack held it, and the giant woke up. Quickly Jack ran out of the giant's house as fast as he could. But now the giant was wide awake and ran after him.

Jack leapt onto the beanstalk and started to climb down. The hen kept clucking and the giant was getting closer.

As Jack got nearer to the bottom, he shouted, "Mother, mother! Quickly, bring me an axe!"

144

Jack and the Beanstalk

Jack was nearly on the ground when his mother came out of the house with an axe. She had the shock of her life when she saw Jack coming down the beanstalk followed by the angry giant.

Jack quickly jumped off the beanstalk and with two big strikes of the axe, chopped the beanstalk down. The giant and the beanstalk came toppling

down together in one big heap.
Jack gave his mother the
golden hen. For the rest of their
lives it laid golden eggs. Jack
and his mother became very
rich and one day Jack met a
beautiful princess. She and Jack
were soon married and they all
lived happily ever after.

Tom Thumb

One evening a woodcutter and his wife sat in their cottage. The poor woodcutter's wife said, "I wish I had a child. Even a small child no bigger than my

thumb would make me happy!"
Believe it or not, within the year,
her wish had come true. She
had a little boy who was strong
and healthy, but no bigger than
her thumb! They loved him
dearly and called
him Tom Thumb.

Tom Thumb

One day when Tom was working in the woods with his father, two strangers passed by and saw how tiny Tom was.

"People would pay us good money to see such a strange little man. He could make us rich!" the strangers said. They offered the poor woodcutter money for his son.

Although the woodcutter didn't want to sell him, Tom

promised his father he would come home one day, so he set off with the strangers.

When it got dark, Tom saw his chance and escaped by running into a mouse hole. The strangers

searched and searched but they couldn't find him, so they left.

Tom was free, but he was a long way from home and felt frightened all alone in the woods. And then, suddenly, with one quick snap, Tom was caught and eaten by a huge hungry wolf.

"My good friend," Tom said from inside the wolf's tummy, "I know where there's a cottage with a pantry full of food." The wolf was surprised someone was talking to him from inside his tummy. But he was still very hungry, so he listened.

"Where is this place full of food?" asked the wolf. Tom told the wolf where his home was. "You can crawl through a drain into the pantry," said Tom.

So the wolf ran all the way to Tom's home. When it got there, the wolf crawled through a drain into the pantry and found ham, beef, cold chicken, cakes and apples. The wolf ate and ate until it was stuffed full!

When the wolf had eaten all he could, he tried to leave, but he couldn't fit through the drain because he was too fat!

Inside the wolf, Tom shouted as loud as he could and woke the woodcutter and his wife. They came downstairs to see what all the noise was.

When they opened the pantry door, Tom cried, "Father! Mother! I'm inside the wolf's tummy!" So the woodcutter killed the wolf and there inside was Tom Thumb.

Tom Thumb

"You're back with us, and we'll never let you go again," said Tom's mother and father. Tom told his parents all about his adventures. "But," he said, "there's no place like home."

Snow White and the Seven Dwarfs

There was once a beautiful young princess called Snow White. Her mother had died and her father had married a new queen, who was beautiful too, but very proud. She didn't want anyone to be prettier than her.

Every day the queen would go to her magic mirror and ask, "Mirror, mirror, on the wall. Who is the fairest of them all?" And the mirror would answer, "You, my queen are the fairest of them all!"

As Snow White grew up, she became more beautiful. One day when the queen asked her mirror who was the fairest of them all, it said, "You, my queen are fair, but Snow White is the fairest of them all."

The queen was furious. She told a servant to take Snow White into the woods and kill her.

The servant led Snow White away, but he couldn't kill her. Instead, he left her in the woods and returned to the palace. He pretended he had done as the queen had asked.

Snow White was frightened in the woods and walked for a long time. After a while, she found a cottage and knocked on the door. There was no answer, so Snow White went in.

Everything was very small and neat inside. There was a table set with seven little plates and seven little glasses. Snow White saw seven cosy little beds, so she lay down on

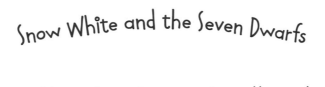

one of the beds and fell asleep.
Soon the seven little dwarfs
who lived in the cottage came
home. They found Snow White
asleep and gently woke her. She
told the dwarfs all about the
cruel queen.

The dwarfs were kind and let Snow White stay with them. So she looked after the cottage, cooked and cleaned while the dwarfs went to work.

After a few weeks the queen again asked her magic mirror who was the fairest in the land. She was shocked to hear, "Snow White, who lives in the woods with the seven dwarfs, is fairer than you."

The nasty queen made a plan to poison Snow White. Then she dressed as an old lady and went to the cottage.

The queen knocked at the door pretending to sell apples. She offered Snow White an

apple – but she had filled one side with poison! The dwarfs had told Snow White to be extra careful. Snow White said, "I'm sorry, but I can't take anything from strangers."

Then the queen took a bite out of the apple to show Snow White it would not hurt her. But of course she had eaten from the side with no poison.

Then the queen gave Snow

White the side of the apple with the poison. As soon as Snow White took a bite, she fell to the floor. The wicked queen smiled and left the cottage.

Later, when the dwarfs came home they found Snow White lying on the ground. She didn't move or breathe, and they thought she was dead.

The dwarfs felt so sad. They made a glass case for Snow

White. They put her in the case and placed it in a pretty spot in the woods. Snow White looked just like she was sleeping.

One day a prince was riding in the woods and he saw Snow White in the glass case. As he

leaned against the glass to look closer, he knocked the case. The piece of poison apple fell out of Snow White's mouth.

Snow White woke up and looked around her. She saw the prince and asked who he was. "You will be safe with me," the prince said, and took Snow White back to his palace.

Meanwhile, the wicked queen again asked her magic mirror,

"Tell me mirror, who is the fairest of them all?"

Her mirror answered, "Snow White is the fairest of them all." The queen was so angry that she burst into flames!

Snow White and the prince were soon married and they lived happily ever after.

The Selfish Giant

Often, on the way home from school, the children stopped to play in the giant's garden. The giant had been away from home for seven years, so the children felt quite safe playing in the lovely big garden. It had soft, green grass, flowers that looked like colourful stars and tall trees with tasty fruit.

But one day the giant came home, and he saw the children. "What are you doing in my garden?" he said grumpily.

He didn't want anyone else in his garden, so the giant built a high wall around it. He also put

up a sign that said "Keep Out!"
Now the poor children had
nowhere to play. What a selfish
giant he was.

Spring came and there were birds and blossom everywhere, except in the giant's garden. The birds didn't go in the garden when there were no children to drop crumbs for them.

Once, a beautiful flower popped its head out from the grass. But when it saw the sign, it slipped back into the ground again and went off to sleep.

The only things that were

pleased to go into the giant's garden were the snow and the frost. Snow covered the grass white and the frost painted the trees silver.

The selfish giant looked out over his cold, white garden. He couldn't understand why spring was so late. But spring didn't come to the giant's garden, and neither did summer, or autumn.

One morning, the giant was

173

lying in bed when he heard the most beautiful music. It was a bird singing outside his window, but it had been so long since he'd heard a bird singing, he had forgotten how lovely it could sound.

The giant looked out of his window.

The Selfish Giant

He saw that some children had crept through a little hole in his wall. They were sitting in the trees, and the trees were so glad to have the children back they had covered themselves in blossom. Birds were twittering with delight and the flowers were peeping up through the green grass. The giant's

175

heart melted. 'I've been so selfish!' he thought to himself. 'Now I know why spring wouldn't come here.'

So the giant crept downstairs and quietly opened the front door. But when he went into his garden, the children were frightened and ran off.

One little boy didn't see the giant because he was too busy trying to climb a tree. The giant bent down and gently lifted the boy up into the tree. The other children saw that the giant wasn't mean anymore, so they came back into the garden.

"It's your garden now, children," said the giant, and he knocked down the wall and took away the sign.

Thumbelina

Once upon a time a woman planted a magic seed. The seed grew into a stunning flower and inside the flower was a tiny child no bigger

Thumbelina

than the woman's thumb. The
woman named her Thumbelina.
One night while she was
sleeping, a huge toad stole
Thumbelina and
carried her away.

The toad put Thumbelina on a lily pad in the middle of the river. Thumbelina wept in fear as there was water all around and no way to reach land.

The silvery fish in the river felt sorry for Thumbelina and nibbled at the lily pad's stalk. So it broke free and floated away with Thumbelina still on it. It sailed past many towns like a little boat bobbing on the water.

Suddenly, a large beetle grabbed Thumbelina in his claws and flew with her to a tree. But when he showed Thumbelina to his friends, they thought she was a strange-looking beetle and they let her go.

For the rest of the year Thumbelina lived in the forest. When winter came, snowflakes fell on her like heavy stones and she was freezing cold.

One day she found a door
to the house of a field mouse.
"Please can you help me, and
give me some food?" asked
Thumbelina. The field mouse let

Thumbelina into his house and she stayed with him for the rest of the winter.

A mole wearing a smart black coat visited the field mouse during the winter. He told Thumbelina not to go into one of his tunnels, because there was a dead bird there. But Thumbelina visited the bird anyway. She felt sorry for it, and made it a blanket out of hay. But as she laid it over the bird she saw it move. He was only frozen and not dead at all!

For the rest of the winter Thumbelina looked after the poorly bird. She didn't tell the mole or the field mouse and by spring, the bird was well enough to fly. Thumbelina waved him goodbye with tears in her eyes.

By this time the mole had grown fond of Thumbelina and

decided she should stay with
him and live underground.
Thumbelina didn't want to live
underground with the mole. She
would miss the sun's warmth,
the flowers and birdsong. But
didn't feel she had a choice.

Thumbelina went outside one
last time to feel the air on her
face and to hear the birds.
Suddenly, she heard a different
song. It was her friend the bird!

"Fly with me, my dear little one," he said. "You saved my life, and now I can help you."

Thumbelina was overjoyed, and escaped with the bird. They flew far away to a land full of tiny people, just like Thumbelina, all living in beautiful flowers.

There Thumbelina met a handsome prince who gave her a pair of glittering wings, so

186

she could fly from flower to flower too.

In this new land, Thumbelina was happier than she had ever been. It wasn't long before she married the prince and they lived happily ever after.

The Elves and the Shoemaker

There was once a poor man who worked hard making shoes. One day he found that he only had enough material left for one more pair of shoes.

The Elves and the Shoemaker

The shoemaker cut out the material and left it ready for the next day. You can imagine his surprise in the morning when he found the shoes already made! They were so beautifully sewn he could hardly see the stitches. They were the most stunning shoes he had ever seen.

That day a customer came into the shoemaker's shop. She tried the shoes on, loved them and paid the shoemaker a good price. Now the shoemaker had enough money to buy material for two more pairs of shoes.

In the evening the shoemaker

set everything out as before and
went up to bed. When he came
downstairs to his shop in the
morning, two splendid pairs of
shoes had been made!

Two customers loved the
shoes so much they paid a huge
amount of money for them. The
shoemaker bought even more
material, and so it went on.

Every evening the shoemaker
left everything set out, and

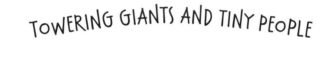

every morning the shoes were already made. Soon the shoemaker had grown rich.

One evening, the shoemaker said to his wife, "Let's stay up to see who's making our

shoes." So they hid behind a curtain in the corner of the workshop.

As the clock struck midnight, two little elves in tatty clothes appeared and began to make the shoes. Their little fingers were stitching and tapping so fast the shoemaker couldn't take his eyes off them.

The little elves worked hard all night until they had finished the shoes. Then, just as quickly as they had appeared, they disappeared again.

The next morning the shoemaker's wife said, "Those little elves have helped us and made us rich. We must do something for them." And the shoemaker said, "Did you notice their clothes were tatty? Let's make them some tiny clothes."

So his wife made the little elves some shirts, coats and trousers, and the shoemaker made them some tiny shoes. They left the clothes on the workbench and hid behind the curtain again.

At midnight when the elves

arrived, they found their new clothes. They put everything on and were so happy, they hopped

196

and skipped around the room.

The shoemaker and his wife didn't see the elves anymore after that. But they had made enough money and were never poor again.

AMAZING ADVENTURES

Dick Whittington and His Cat 200

Little Red Riding Hood 209

Trains, Planes, Boats and Trucks 218

Off To Play Music in Bremen 227

The Queen Bee 234

The Ugly Duckling 246

Dick Whittington and His Cat

Hundreds of years ago there lived a poor boy called Dick. His mother and father died when he was young, so he was left an orphan.

One day Dick heard the villagers talking about a big, grand city called London. He heard there was singing and music all day long and the streets were made of gold.

Dick thought he would try his luck in London. So one day he and his cat got a lift to London in a man's wagon. When they arrived Dick looked everywhere for the streets made of gold,

but he found nothing but dirt!
For many days and nights Dick
and his cat lived out on the
streets, eating scraps of food.

At last Dick was so tired and
hungry that he lay down in the
doorway of a big house. As luck
would have it Dick had chosen
the doorway of a rich and kind
gentleman called Mr Fitzwarren.

"Why are you lying there,
lazy lad?" said Mr Fitzwarren

when he saw him.

"I'm not lazy," said Dick.
"With all my heart I would
work, but I'm weak because I'm

203

hungry." So Mr Fitzwarren said Dick and his cat could live and work in his home.

Dick worked hard and everyone liked him, except the cook. She was always giving Dick the worst jobs to do.

One day Mr Fitzwarren's ship was due to set sail, and everyone in his household gave a small gift to the ship for good luck. All Dick owned was his cat,

so he sadly handed her over.

The people on the ship laughed at Dick's gift, but once they were at sea they were glad to have her. There were lots of mice and rats on the ship that ate their food, but Dick's cat chased and ate them all!

During the voyage, there were fierce storms at sea and the ship was blown to a faraway island. The people living there

were pleased to have visitors, and their king invited everyone from the ship to a grand feast.

But as soon as the dishes of food were set out, rats rushed over the tables and ate it all up.

"I will give gold to anyone who can get rid of these rats,"

the king cried. The ship's captain remembered Dick's cat and quickly fetched her.

The cat immediately chased all the rats into the sea. The king was overjoyed! He asked the captain if he could keep the cat, and as payment gave him a big pile of gold.

The ship sailed home where the captain gave Dick a share of the fortune.

Dick missed his cat, but he was pleased to hear she was happy chasing rats for the King.

While the ship had been at see, Dick and Mr Fitzwarren's daughter had fallen in love. Soon they were married and had lots of children, and lots of cats!

Little Red Riding Hood

Once upon a time there was a little girl who lived in a village with her mother. Her grandmother made her a red coat with a hood. The little girl

wore her coat so much that
everyone called her Little Red
Riding Hood.

One day her mother said,
"Your grandmother is ill. Please
take this basket of food to her."
So Little Red Riding Hood put
on her red coat and set off
through the wood to her
grandmother's house.

As she was walking she met
a wolf. The wolf was hungry, but

he didn't dare eat Little Red
Riding Hood, because there were
woodcutters working nearby.

The wolf asked her where
she was going, and Little Red
Riding Hood, forgetting that she
shouldn't talk to strangers, told
the wolf she was going to visit
her grandmother.

Leaving Little Red Riding
Hood on the path, the wolf took
a shortcut through the wood to

Little Red Riding Hood

Granny's house and tapped on the door. Thinking it was Little Red Riding Hood, Granny opened it. The wolf immediately leapt on Granny, shut her in the wardrobe, put on her spare nightclothes and got into bed.

Soon after, Little Red Riding Hood reached Granny's house. She knocked on the door. The wolf, who was pretending to be Granny, told her to come in.

Little Red Riding Hood wondered why her grandmother sounded strange, but thought it must be because she wasn't well.

The little girl walked in and over to Granny's bed. She was surprised at how she looked, and said, "Granny, what big ears you have!"

"All the better to hear you with, my dear," said the wolf.

"What big eyes you have!" said Little Red Riding Hood.

"All the better to see you with," said the wolf.

"And what enormous teeth you have!" said Little Red Riding Hood peering closer.

"All the better to EAT you

with!" cried the wolf, and leapt towards Little Red Riding Hood, who screamed loudly.

Luckily, a woodcutter working nearby heard the scream and burst into Granny's house. He

chased the nasty wolf out of the house with his axe. Then the woodcutter and Little Red Riding Hood found Granny in the wardrobe and let her out.

Then they all sat down to eat the food Little Red Riding Hood had brought – and the wolf was never seen again.

Trains, Planes, Boats and Trucks

At night time, when little girls and boys are all asleep, their toys often like to come out to play, and to visit each other. One night a group of toys had a delightful picnic in their friend's new playroom. Soon, it was time to go home, so they all said goodnight to each other and got on board a little toy train to go back to their own playroom.

Tama Teddy found a quiet carriage to sit in and soon fell fast asleep. She didn't feel the train go outside, or stop at their doll's house. She didn't know the train had gone far across town.

It was only when the train
stopped at the end of the line
that Tama Teddy woke up.
Imagine her shock when she
found out she was the only toy
on the train and far from home!

The train didn't go back until
the next day so Tama had
to find another way home.
She left the train

and walked into a small garden, where she met Ruby Ragdoll.

Ruby saw Tama looking sad. "Are you ok?" Ruby asked. Tama told Ruby what had happened. "I can take you some of the way," said Ruby, and led Tama to a shiny, red plane. "I'm flying to the next town and I can take you there."

So Tama climbed on board and closed her eyes.

She was feeling quite scared,
but when she opened
her eyes, they
were flying
high up in the
sky. The fields
below looked
so tiny.

Ruby's plane whizzed through
the sky and in no time they had
landed in the next town. It was
a big town with a river running

through it.

Ruby told Tama to head for the river. "Robbie Robot has a boat and he can help you," said Ruby. So Tama Teddy thanked Ruby and walked down towards the river.

"I'd be happy to give you a lift in my boat," said Robbie.

"But I'm only going as far as the next town." So Tama climbed on board Robbie's boat and they chugged along the river to the next town.

Robbie told Tama that Pedro Puppet would be able to help

her because he had a car. But when Tama found Pedro he said he didn't have a car – he had an old, rusty truck.

Tama didn't think Pedro's truck would get very far. "I've driven many miles in my truck and it's never broken down." said Pedro. But they hadn't gone very far, when... kerplunk. Something fell off the truck!

"Oh no! What's happened?"

cried Tama. "We've lost a wheel!" said Pedro. Tama didn't think she'd ever get home now.

But as they coasted with a rattle and a clonk down a hill, Tama looked up at a nearby window, and saw... the doll's house. She was home at last!

Off to Play Music in Bremen

There was once a donkey who carried heavy corn sacks to the mill. But as the donkey got older he found the work harder to do. One day he ran away and set off to a town called Bremen. 'I will play music in Bremen,' the donkey thought.

On the way to Bremen, Donkey met a dog by the roadside. Dog told him that he was getting old too and could no longer herd sheep.

"Come with me to Bremen," said Donkey. "I will play the flute and you can beat a drum." Dog was delighted with Donkey's offer and agreed to go with him.

Soon the two animals met a cat. "I'm getting old and can no longer catch mice," said Cat. "Come and play music with us in Bremen," said Donkey and Dog, and off they went together.

Shortly after the friends came to a farm where a cockerel was crowing loudly. "What's the matter?" asked Donkey. The cockerel told them he was going to be eaten the next day. "You have a good voice. Why not come with us to Bremen?" asked Donkey. The Cockerel happily agreed.

The four friends continued on their way, and that evening they reached a forest. They decided to look for somewhere to sleep.

Cockerel spotted a light far off in the forest. The friends headed towards the light and

Off to Play Music in Bremen

found it came from a cottage on a hill. They peeped in through the window and saw four thieves sitting at the table, about to eat their supper.

"How can we chase the thieves away?" said Dog. Then Donkey had an idea.

At Donkey's signal, they began to sing outside the cottage. Donkey brayed, Dog barked, Cat mewed and Cockerel crowed. It was such a dreadful din!

The thieves were terrified by the noise. They covered their ears and ran out of the cottage. They were so scared they never dared to go back. The four friends liked the cottage so much that they never left. They carried on making music, but they never did get to Bremen.

The Queen Bee

Once upon a time there were three princes. The two oldest princes set off into the world to have adventures, but they did silly things, wasted their money and came home.

When the youngest prince was old enough he wanted to go on adventures with his brothers. They laughed at him and said, "We know a lot, and we've still made a mess of things. Why do you think you can do better?" They called their little brother Prince Silly-Billy. However, the three princes set off on their next journey together.

They soon came to an anthill. The two older princes wanted to tear it down, but Prince Silly-Billy said, "Don't be mean. Leave the ants alone!" So the princes carried on walking.

Next, they came to a lake with a lot of ducks paddling about. The older princes wanted to catch two of the ducks and cook them for dinner. But Prince Silly-Billy said, "Leave the

The Queen Bee

ducks alone. Don't kill them!"
Further along the road, the brothers found a nest of bees in a tree. Tasty honey from the nest ran down the tree

trunk. The oldest princes wanted to kill the bees and eat all the honey. The youngest prince stopped them again.

Later that day, the three princes came to a creepy castle. There were many stone statues in the castle, but the only person they met was a little, old man.

The old man said to the eldest prince, "A thousand pearls are hidden in the woods. Find all

the pearls by the end of the day, or you'll be turned into stone." The eldest prince thought it would be easy to find the pearls, but by the end of the day he had only found a handful, so he was turned into stone.

Next, the second eldest prince went to look for the pearls in the woods. He was sure he'd do better than his brother, but he couldn't find

many of the pearls, either. So
he was also turned into stone.
    At last it was Prince Silly-
Billy's turn to go into the woods.
He had only found a few of the
pearls when suddenly, along
came all the ants he'd saved

earlier. They'd come to help, and very quickly found all the pearls.

The old man said Prince Silly-Billy had done well. "But the test is not over," he went on. "Now you must find the key to the princess's room. The key is

at the bottom of the lake."

Prince Silly-Billy went to the edge of the lake, but didn't know how he could ever find the key. His heart sank, but just then, the two ducks he had saved earlier came to help. They dived to the bottom of the lake and brought back the key.

The old man took Prince Silly-Billy inside, where three princesses were sleeping.

"You must guess which is the youngest princess to break the spell and wake them," the old man said. The princesses all looked the same age. Prince Silly-Billy didn't know how he would guess who was the youngest princess. Just then the bees he'd saved earlier came to his rescue.

The Queen Bee remembered the youngest princess had eaten

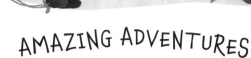

some honey
before the
spell was put
on her. So
the Queen
Bee landed
on the lips of
each princess,
and tasted honey on the lips of
one of them. This was the
youngest princess.

The Queen Bee told Prince

Silly-Billy, and when he guessed right, the spell was broken. The two elder princes, and everyone in the castle who had been turned to stone, woke up.

Prince Silly-Billy married the youngest princess and his brothers never dared laugh at him again.

The Ugly Duckling

One fine summer's day Mother Duck was waiting for her eggs to hatch. Suddenly one shell cracked, and then another, and another. Slowly, bit

by bit, little fluffy ducklings
began to stick their heads out
of their shells. "Peep, peep!"

After a while, Mother Duck
looked in her nest. "Are you all
out?" she asked. But the largest
egg still hadn't cracked open.

Old Duck asked how Mother
Duck was doing. "There's one
egg still to hatch," said Mother
Duck. "But just look at my other
pretty ducklings."

At last the largest egg
cracked open and out fell...
a big, grey ugly duckling. He
looked nothing like his
brothers and sisters.

Mother Duck
took her family
to the pond on
the farm.
She jumped
into the
water with

a splash. One after the other her ducklings jumped in after her and paddled their little legs to keep up with their mother.

Next Mother Duck took her ducklings around the farm. The other animals laughed at her biggest duckling. He wasn't fluffy or yellow, and he was quite clumsy too. Mother Duck told them to leave him alone, but as the days went by it got worse.

The other ducks pecked at him, and even his brothers and sisters called him names.

So at last the ugly duckling ran away. He ducked under a fence into a field, where he met some wild ducks and geese, but they were mean to him too.

The duckling left the field and found a pond to swim in. He spent many months there, but felt very lonely because he

always tried to stay away from other animals.

Winter came and it got colder and colder. The pond water began to freeze, until one morning the ugly duckling woke up and realized he was completely stuck in the ice.

Luckily, a man found him just in time. He broke the ice and freed the duckling. So the ugly duckling stayed with the man all

winter. By spring, the duckling felt better and was able to live outside again.

The ugly duckling loved the warm sun and the singing birds. He was growing stronger every day. He flapped his wings against his sides and, before he knew what was happening, he flew high into the sky.

As he looked down, he could see some beautiful swans on a

lake below. The duckling was afraid to fly down to them, 'They won't like me because I'm ugly,' he thought. But then a strange thing happened – the swans came to meet him.

As the duckling flew down to the water, he caught sight of himself in its reflection. He wasn't a clumsy, ugly duckling anymore. He was a graceful and beautiful swan.

The Ugly Duckling

STRANGE SPELLS

Rumplestiltskin 258

Snow-White and Rose-Red 272

The Three Dogs 284

The Hut in the Woods 293

Sizzle, Drizzle, Thudd and Dudd 301

Rapunzel 310

Rumplestiltskin

Once upon a time there was a poor miller who had a very beautiful daughter. One day the miller met the King and told him a boastful fib.

Rumplestiltskin

"My daughter can spin straw into gold," said the miller. So the king asked the miller to bring his daughter to the palace.

The king showed the girl into a room filled with straw and gave her a spinning wheel. "Spin this straw into gold by morning or you'll be killed," he told her. Then he locked her in the room.

The girl was frightened and began to cry. How could she

turn the straw into gold?

Suddenly, the door opened and a strange little man walked in. He asked the girl why she was crying and she told him. "What will you give me if I spin the straw into gold for you?" asked the man. So the girl gave him her necklace. The man sat down and started spinning. Whirr, whirr went the spinning wheel. He spun

Rumplestiltskin

all night until all the straw in the room had been turned into gold.

In the morning, the King was amazed to find the room filled with gold. The King was greedy though, so he took the girl into a bigger room filled with straw.

Again he said, "Spin this straw into gold by the morning, or you will be killed," and he locked her in the room.

The girl didn't Know what to

do and was crying when the door opened. The little man walked in and said, "What will you give me if I spin the straw into gold?" This time the girl gave the man her ring.

The little man sat down and started spinning for a second time. Whirr, whirr – he spun all night until all the straw in the room was spun into gold.

The king couldn't believe his

eyes the next morning, when he saw the room filled with gold. But it still wasn't enough, so he took the girl to an even bigger room filled with straw. "If you spin this straw into gold by morning, you will be my wife," he said.

When the girl had been left alone in walked the little man again. This time, however, the girl had nothing left to give him. The man said, "If you marry the King, you must give me your first child." The girl agreed and the man spun all night, turning the huge pile of straw into gold.

When the King discovered that all the straw in the last room had been spun into gold, he married the miller's daughter. She became queen, and a year later she had a child.

Within days, the little man appeared and asked the queen for her child. But the queen didn't want to give up her baby.

Rumplestiltskin

"I will give you three days to guess my name," the man said. And if you guess it, you can keep your child."

So the queen thought of all the names she had ever heard. When the little man came to see her the next day, she tried them all, one after another. To every name the man said, "That is not my name."

On the second day, the queen

asked people living near the palace for their names. She repeated them all to the little man – even the most unusual ones. "Is it Shortribs? Sheepshanks? Lacelegs?" she asked. But he always answered, "That is not my name."

Next day, the queen sent out messengers to find more names. Near the end of the day, one messenger returned and told

the queen of a strange little
man he had seen singing and
dancing around a fire.

The messenger repeated the
man's song:

STRANGE SPELLS

It's time to sing and to go wild,
For soon I'll have the queen's
first child.
She'll never win my little game,
For Rumplestiltskin is my name!

You can imagine how pleased
the queen was to hear this.
Soon after the messenger had
left, the little man appeared.
The queen said, "Is your name...
Rumplestiltskin?"

Rumplestiltskin

The little man went red in the face. He was *so* angry that the queen had finally guessed his name. "Someone told you!" he shouted in fury. He stamped his feet so hard that the ground split underneath him. It swallowed him up, and he was never, ever seen again.

Snow-White and Rose-Red

Once upon a time there was a poor woman who lived in a cottage with her two daughters. In their garden, they had two rose trees – one with white

roses and the other with red.
The rose trees were like the
two daughters, who were called
Snow-White and Rose-Red.

One evening as the family
was sitting by their fire, they
heard a knock at the cottage
door. On the doorstep stood a
big, black bear. Rose-Red
screamed and Snow-White hid
behind her mother. "Don't be
scared," said the bear. "I won't

hurt you. I would just like to warm up by your fire."

So the mother invited the bear in and soon he was comfortable, and laughing with the girls. At bedtime, the bear slept by the fire and in the morning he left. Every evening after that, the bear stayed the night in the cottage.

One morning, the bear said he was going away for a while. Snow-White was sorry the bear was leaving, but she let him out of the cottage. As he left, a little of his black fur caught on the door. Snow-White thought she saw gold under the fur.

Some time later Snow-White and Rose-Red went to

the forest to fetch firewood. They saw a dwarf with his beard trapped in a fallen log. "Why are you standing there? Help me!" said the dwarf angrily.

Snow-White pulled some scissors out of her pocket and cut off the bit of the dwarf's beard that was trapped.

But the dwarf didn't thank Snow-White for setting him free. Instead he shouted, "You silly girl! You've cut off some of my fine beard!" He picked up a bag of gold and stormed off.

Later the girls met the angry dwarf again. This time his beard was caught in a fishing line. Again Snow-White cut off the end of his beard to free him, and again the dwarf didn't thank her, but stormed off clutching a bag of pearls.

The next day the girls went into town to buy some ribbons. A huge eagle flew down ahead of them and they heard a loud cry. They raced over to see what had happened. To their amazement they found that the big bird was trying to carry off the dwarf. So the girls grabbed hold of the dwarf and pulled and pulled until the eagle finally let him go.

The girls had saved the dwarf again, but still he didn't thank them. "You've torn my coat, you clumsy girls!" he cried. Then he grabbed a sack of jewels, and left.

The girls didn't think they'd see the dwarf again. But on their way home, there he was in

STRANGE SPELLS

the wood counting his treasure!
"What are you looking at?"
grumbled the dwarf.
Suddenly there was
a growl and a black
bear appeared.

"Don't eat me!" shouted the dwarf. "Eat the girls who are bigger and tastier than me!"

But the huge bear didn't take any notice of the dwarf. He growled again, and then hit the dwarf so hard with his giant paw that the grumpy little man went flying up, up, up into the air. No one ever found out where he landed.

The girls were frightened

until they saw it was their own friendly bear. As they watched, the bear started to shed his fur, until standing in front of them was a smiling handsome prince. "At last, the dwarf's spell has been broken," he said. Then the prince collected up the treasure the dwarf had stolen and took both girls back to his palace.

Over time, the prince fell hopelessly in love with Snow-

Snow-White and Rose-Red

White, while not long after
Rose-Red married his younger
brother. The girl's mother came
to live with them in the palace
and brought her roses with her.
The two rose trees bloomed big,
bright and beautiful with white
and red roses every year.

The Three Dogs

Once upon a time there was a shepherd. When he died he left his three sheep to his son. The son set off with the sheep to look for work, but he

The Three Dogs

couldn't find any. Exhausted, he sat down at the side of the road with his sheep, feeling grumpy.

Suddenly, a strange man with three dogs appeared. "Hello, I'll swap my three dogs for your three sheep," the man said. He told the son that his dogs were magic. "The smallest dog is called Salt. He will bring you food. The middle-sized dog is called Pepper. He will stop

anyone hurting you. The biggest
dog is Mustard. He's so strong
he can break iron bars in his
teeth," said the man.

So the son swapped his
three sheep for the

man's three dogs. To test the dogs he said, "Salt, I'm hungry," and before the words were out of his mouth, the dog ran off and returned with a big basket full of delicious food.

The next day, a carriage driven by a coachman stopped on the road by the son. A beautiful princess was crying inside the carriage. The son asked her what was wrong. She told him that every year a princess was fed to a dragon, and this year it was her turn.

The son felt sorry for the princess so he went with her to face the dragon. It was a huge monster with enormous wings and sharp talons! As it flew towards them, the son cried, "Pepper, help me."

Immediately, the middle-sized dog leapt on the dragon and

killed it. The son picked up two of the dragon's teeth and put them in his pocket. The princess begged him to come with her to the palace, but the son wished to see more of the world first.

Now the coachman who had been driving the princess's carriage was a wicked man. He told the princess to tell the king that it was he who had killed the dragon. The princess was frightened, so she did as he asked. The King thought the coachman was a brave man and agreed he deserved to marry the princess.

A few days before the wedding, the son journeyed to the palace. He tried to explain that he had killed the dragon, but the

The Three Dogs

coachman threw him into prison.
Left alone, the son called out,
"Mustard, help me!" In a flash,
the biggest dog began chewing
through the bars of the window.

As soon as he was
free, the son went to
the King, and the
princess agreed to tell
the true story. Then the
son showed the King the
two dragon teeth, so he

knew he was telling the truth.

The coachman was thrown in prison, and the son and the princess were married. Soon after, the dogs said, "Our work is done. You don't need us now." Then they turned into three birds and flew away.

The Hut in the Woods

A poor woodcutter lived in a hut on the edge of the woods with his wife and three daughters. One morning the woodcutter said to his wife,

STRANGE SPELLS

"Tell our eldest daughter to bring my lunch today." To show her the way through the woods, the woodcutter dropped some seeds on the ground.

At lunchtime the eldest daughter set off, but birds had eaten all the seeds, and she was soon lost. As it grew dark she became frightened but then she saw a hut.

The Hut in the Woods

She bravely knocked on the door, and was invited inside by an old man with a long white beard. He lived in the hut with a hen, a cockerel and a cow. The man said the girl could stay the night if she cooked dinner.

So she cooked a tasty dinner for the man and herself, but

forgot to feed the animals. The
man opened a trapdoor, and
with a cry, the girl slid down a
tunnel into a cold cellar.

The next morning the
woodcutter said to his wife, "Our
first daughter is missing. Tell
our second daughter to find her,
and to bring my lunch to me on
the way." This time he dropped
some lentils to show the way
through the woods.

But when his second daughter set off, the birds had eaten the lentils too. The second daughter was soon lost and came to the house belonging to the old man.

She was also asked to cook dinner and she, too, forgot the animals and ended up in the cold, dark cellar.

On the third morning the woodcutter said to his wife, "Send our youngest daughter to find her sisters, and bring my lunch on her way." He laid a trail of peas for her to follow. But pigeons ate the peas and that daughter was soon lost too.

At last she reached the hut in the woods. Like her sisters before her, she was asked to cook dinner.

Now, the youngest daughter was kind and gentle. So she fed, watered and cared for the animals before she made dinner. When she woke the next morning she was shocked to find herself in a huge palace.

The old man had turned into a handsome prince. He told her, "A witch changed me into an old man, but you broke the spell with your good, kind heart. You showed love towards the animals as well as to me."

The prince and his new princess lived happily in the palace. Her sisters were set free, but they weren't invited to the palace until they had learned to be kinder to animals.

Sizzle, Drizzle, Thudd and Dudd

There was once a boy called Storm who thought he was the best at everything. He told everyone he was the best.

He would steal all the paints

and finish his painting first. Then he would shout, "My painting is the best!" Or he would push everyone away from the slide, climb up first and shout, "I'm the best on the slide!" as he was sliding down.

Wizard Thunder had been watching Storm for a while and thought it was time he taught him a lesson.

One day when Storm was

Sizzle, Drizzle, Thudd and Dudd

playing football with his friends, the wizard waved his magic wand and said, "Sizzle, drizzle, thudd and dudd, make Storm's feet stuck in the mud!"

In a flash, Storm's feet were stuck in thick, gooey mud. He pulled and pulled, but he couldn't move. His friend Tumble got to the ball first and scored a goal. Storm felt cross when everyone cheered Tumble.

Then, the next day Storm and his friends were racing their bicycles. Storm was near the finish and about to say he was the best rider, when the wizard waved his magic wand. "Sizzle, drizzle, lords and swords, make Storm's wheels go backwards!"

In a flash, Storm's bicycle

wheels went backwards, so all his friends finished before he did. Storm felt angry that his friends had beaten him.

On the third day, Storm and his friends Tumble and Star were flying a kite in the garden. The kite came down in next door's garden, so Storm and Star ran off to peep over the wall. Mrs Green, the neighbour, was sitting in the garden, but she wasn't looking their way.

Storm opened his mouth to shout to Mrs Green. But the wizard said, "Sizzle, drizzle, round and round, take away all Storm's sound!" As Storm opened his mouth to speak, no sound came out. He tried again, but he couldn't say a word.

Star saw that Storm needed help. So in her bravest and biggest voice she shouted,

"Mrs Green, please can we have our kite back?"

Mrs Green heard Star and threw the children's kite back to them. But Storm snatched it up and raced away. He wanted Tumble to think that he'd got the kite back on his own.

But then Storm saw Star's sad face, and he knew what he was doing was wrong. It was Star who had asked for their kite back. She was the real hero.

Storm stopped running around with the kite and handed it over to Star with a smile. Then they raced back down the garden again, and Star told Tumble she had got the kite back. Storm felt really happy for her.

Wizard Thunder saw that Storm had learnt his lesson. He waved his magic wand one more time and said, "Sizzle, drizzle, round and round, this time give Storm back his sound!" And the first words Storm said were, "You're the best, Star!"

Rapunzel

Long ago a man and a woman lived next to a witch. The witch's garden was full of tasty vegetables. The woman was expecting a baby and she

longed to eat some of the lettuces. One day she persuaded her husband to get her some.

Even though he was afraid, he climbed over the garden wall and took some of the lettuces.

STRANGE SPELLS

His wife thought the lettuce was delicious and begged her husband for more. But the next time the husband climbed over the wall the witch was waiting for him on the other side.

The witch was furious, but the man told her that his wife was pregnant and desperate for some lettuce. Eventually the witch agreed that the man could take some to his wife, as long as the witch could see the child when it was born.

Soon enough, a baby girl called Rapunzel was born, but when the witch came to see the child, she stole her away and locked her up in a tall tower.

Rapunzel grew up into a kind and beautiful girl with long, long golden hair. The tower she lived in had no door or stairs, just a little window at the top. When the witch visited, she would say, "Rapunzel, Rapunzel, Let down your hair." And Rapunzel would throw her long, thick plait out of the window like a rope, so the witch could climb up her hair.

One day, many years later, a prince rode past the tower. He heard Rapunzel's beautiful singing and tried to climb up to her, but he couldn't find a door.

The prince came back every

day to listen to Rapunzel singing.
Then one day, he heard the
witch asking Rapunzel to throw
down her hair.

The prince saw the witch
climb Rapunzel's plait, so when
the witch had gone, he did the
same and climbed up the tower.

At first Rapunzel was
frightened – the witch was the
only person she'd ever seen
before. But the prince spoke to

her softly and she realized he was a kind, young man.

The prince visited Rapunzel the next day, and every day after that. Soon Rapunzel and the prince had fallen in love and wanted to marry. But how could she leave the tower?

The prince had an idea. "Every day I will bring you a piece of silk. Then you will be able to make yourself a ladder,"

he said. So each visit the prince brought a little piece of silk, and the ladder grew longer and longer. But one day Rapunzel

318

forgot to keep the prince a secret. When she was pulling up the witch, she said, "You are much heavier than the prince."

The witch cried, "You have tricked me!" In her anger she cut Rapunzel's plait off and sent her far away.

Later that day when the prince called for Rapunzel to let down her hair, the wicked witch let down Rapunzel's plait. The prince climbed up, but the witch was waiting. She pushed him from the tower and he fell into a thorn bush, which scratched his eyes and made him blind.

For many years the blind prince wondered in the forest. At last he reached the place where Rapunzel had been sent. He heard some beautiful singing and knew it was Rapunzel.

They fell crying into each

other's arms, and as Rapunzel's tears fell on the prince's eyes, he could see again.

The prince took Rapunzel back to his palace and they were married, and lived happily ever after.

MAGICAL LANDS

The Fairy Fluffikins 324

Aladdin 333

The Magic Fiddle 343

The Snow Queen 351

The Crystal Ball 366

Ozma and the Little Wizard 375

323

The Fairy
Fluffikins

Fairy Fluffikins lived in a warm, cosy nest in a hole in the middle of a big oak tree. She wore a little, soft, fluffy brown dress, and a red woolly cap on her head. She had soft red hair and the brightest, naughtiest, merriest brown eyes you could imagine.

Fairy Fluffikins was always up to mischief. She would creep into a nest, where fat baby dormice were sleeping and tickle their toes. The baby dormice would scream with laughter and nearly roll out of bed.

Papa Dormouse would call

out, "You're naughty babies. Go
to sleep at once!" and Fairy
Fluffikins would fly off to look
for more mischief.

One night she found a dead
mouse in a field, and at first she
felt sad for the mouse. But then
Fairy Fluffikins had an idea. She
tied a long piece of grass to its
tail, and then she laid the mouse
on a chopped tree trunk, near
to where Old Owl lived.

Soon she heard a loud voice by the tree saying, "Mmm, I smell mouse!" Fairy Fluffikins waited until Old Owl was about to swoop down, before she quickly pulled the mouse away.

After a while Fairy Fluffikins

gave up teasing Old Owl, and flew off to see what other naughty things she could do.

She found some buttercups to blow on. They thought it was the morning wind waking them up, and opened their cups.

She pulled the tail of a nightingale singing to his love and he fell over backwards into the garden.

Then she spotted an old cat

hunting for mice at night and squeaked like a mouse so the old cat ran after her. Fairy Fluffikins pulled his whiskers, then flew away.

One day when Fairy Fluffikins was flying away from playing yet another naughty trick, she suddenly felt a nip. Old Owl had caught her! As he carried her back to his nest, Fairy Fluffikins cried out, "Please don't be angry with me. I won't play tricks any more."

But Old Owl was angry with Fairy Fluffikins and Mrs Old Owl told her off too. "Now go away you naughty fairy!" so Fairy Fluffikins flew home.

A good while later, Fairy Fluffikins was flying around a haystack looking for something naughty to do. She found a little house with wire walls and an

open door. Fairy Fluffikins hopped into the house and looked around. There was a white thing hanging from the roof, so she pulled it. A door quickly slammed shut and Fairy Fluffikins was caught!

A farmer found her the next

morning, and thought she was a dormouse. He gave her to his daughter who fed her nuts and grains – all the things Fairy Fluffikins didn't like! Now Fairy Fluffikins has no one to tease any more – but maybe that's a good thing.

Aladdin

Once upon a time a boy called Aladdin lived in a place called Persia. One day a tall man arrived at Aladdin's house and introduced himself as his uncle. He asked Aladdin to help him find some treasure.

(However, the man wasn't really Aladdin's uncle, but a mean wizard.) He took Aladdin to a cave and told him to find a gold lamp. The man took a gold ring off his finger and gave it to Aladdin. "This magic ring will help you find the lamp," he said.

So Aladdin bravely went into the cave and found the gold

lamp. But he wouldn't give it to the man until he was allowed out of the cave. "You silly boy!" shouted the man. He muttered some magic words and at once a big rock closed the front of the cave. Aladdin was trapped!

Aladdin felt frightened. He wondered why the lamp was so special, and rubbed off some dirt to get a better look at it. Suddenly, in a puff of smoke a

genie came out of the lamp.
"I am the Genie of the
Lamp. What is it that you wish
for?" he said.

Aladdin

"Get me out of this cave please," said Aladdin, and in a flash Aladdin was home.

Aladdin told his mother all about the man and the lamp in the cave. After that, Aladdin and his mother asked the genie for a great many things and they never wanted for anything.

One day Aladdin saw a lovely princess travelling with her family through the town. He said to the genie, "Please build me a palace of the finest stone to impress the princess. I wish to marry her."

The genie built Aladdin a glittering palace, and when the princess was asked to visit, she was most impressed. Soon after that, Aladdin and the princess were married.

But the wizard came to hear of the marriage. He thought

Aladdin

Aladdin had died in the cave and he was furious that Aladdin had been using his magic lamp all this time.

So, one day the wizard bought a new lamp and went to the palace. He met with the princess and said to her, "I'll give you this new lamp for your old lamp." The princess didn't know that Aladdin's old lamp was magic, so she happily

handed it to the wizard.
The wizard quickly
rubbed the lamp and
told the genie to
move the palace to
Africa! In a puff of
magic, the princess,
the wizard and the
palace vanished.
When Aladdin tried
to return home, he
was shocked to find

Aladdin

the palace had gone.

    Aladdin remembered the magic ring the wizard had given him and asked it to take him to his palace. In a flash, Aladdin was there, and found the princess.

    Together they made a special drink, which the princess gave to the wizard. The drink made him fall into a deep sleep.

As soon as the wizard was snoring, Aladdin grabbed the lamp and asked the genie, "Please, return us to Persia!" Instantly, Aladdin, the princess and the palace were back. They lived happily ever after, and never saw the wizard again.

The Magic Fiddle

Once upon a time there were seven brothers who were all married. They had one sister, but none of the wives liked her. The wives were angry because the sister cooked the most amazing meals. So, one day the wives asked a witch to cast a spell to stop the sister fetching water to cook with.

When the girl put her bucket into the river, the water wouldn't go into the bucket. Instead, it rose up around the girl, creeping up to her knees, then her waist, and getting higher and higher.

The girl cried out, "Help me

brothers. The water is up to my neck!" But no one heard her, and soon she was dragged under the water. The witch took her away and changed her into a bamboo plant.

One day a man passed the bamboo plant and said, "This will make a good fiddle!" He chopped down the bamboo and made it into a fiddle. It was a fine fiddle and people were moved to tears whenever they heard it played.

Everywhere the man went, people would ask, "How much do you want for your fiddle?" But the man didn't want to sell it.

The Magic Fiddle

One day the king asked him to play his fiddle at the palace. The man played beautifully and the king wanted to buy the fiddle for the prince. But again the man wouldn't sell his fiddle.

So the king gave the man a special drink, which made him fall asleep. The king stole the fiddle and gave it to the prince, who kept it locked in his room in the palace.

After that, strange things began to happen. Every day a plate of food would be left under the prince's bed. The prince wondered who was kind enough to be leaving him food.

One day, he hid in the corner of his room to watch. It wasn't long before a beautiful girl stepped out of the fiddle. She combed her hair and then cooked a meal and put it under the prince's bed, before stepping back into the fiddle.

Over the next few days, the prince hid and watched the girl. He thought she was so beautiful and kind, and he fell in love. One day, just as the

349

girl was about to step back into the fiddle, the prince caught her. Straight away he asked her to marry him.

The spell was broken and the girl was free. She married the prince and they lived happily ever after, much to the fury of her brothers' wives.

The Snow Queen

Once upon a time there was a boy and a girl who lived next door to each other. They were called Kay and Gerda, and they were the best of friends.

Every day they played together and talked to each other from their bedroom windows. Everything they did they did together, and told each other all their secrets.

Both Kay and Gerda loved winter, and all the stories Gerda's grandmother told them. Their favourite story was about an evil snow queen, who lived in the hills, in an ice palace. One

The Snow Queen

night, Kay couldn't sleep for
thinking about the Snow Queen,
so he opened his window to lean
out and talk to Gerda about it.

353

But instead of seeing his friend, a magical speck of ice flew into his eye as the Snow Queen soared overhead in her icy, magical sleigh.

From that night, the evil enchantment worked its magic on Kay. He forgot how to be kind and gentle, and people forgot the boy he once was.

Kay was mean to everyone around him and stopped playing

with Gerda altogether. One day
as he played alone in the village,
the Snow Queen came in her
bright white sleigh to take Kay
away to her ice palace.

Later, when Gerda looked for
Kay, no one in the town even
remembered him. But Gerda
was determined not to forget
her friend, and that night she
set off to find him.

She hadn't gone far when

she met a
raven. "I've seen
your friend Kay,"
said the raven, when Gerda
asked him about the Snow

Queen. "They rode past in the sleigh a few days ago. The raven led Gerda deep into a forest and showed her the path to follow, which would take her to the snow palace.

Gerda hadn't gone far when robbers stopped her and, thinking she was rich, took all her belongings and locked her in a nearby barn.

There she met a robber girl,

who looked after the animals belonging to the thieves. Gerda told her all about her search for her friend, Kay.

The robber girl waited until darkness, then helped Gerda on to one of the reindeer kept in the barn. She gave Gerda a

warm cloak and boots, and told
her that the reindeer would
know how to find the ice palace.

Gerda rode through the
overgrown forest for days. The
reindeer climbed steep
slopes and

trudged through snow drifts.
Finally they came to the huge
snow palace.

Gerda was tired and she felt
very scared. But she loved Kay
dearly and missed him, so she
carefully pushed open the
frozen, ice door.

The snow palace was filled
with enormous, shiny blocks of
ice and in the middle of one
huge room sat Kay. He wasn't

moving and he didn't show any signs of recognizing Gerda when she knelt down beside him.

Gerda didn't know what to do. Kay wouldn't move or even look at her. She tried to drag him away from the blocks of ice surrounding him, but he was just too heavy.

Tired and cold, Gerda curled up beside Kay and cried herself to sleep. But something magical started to happen. Gerda's warm tears began to melt the ice crystals deep inside Kay's heart. Gerda's love for her friend was thawing the icy enchantment!

When Gerda awoke, Kay was looking down at her and smiling. There was colour in his cheeks again and he remembered Gerda, and their friendship.

Suddenly, the Snow Queen

appeared in the room. Realizing that the children had defeated her magic, she roared with anger and tried to stop Gerda and Kay from escaping.

But when the Snow Queen reached out to grab Kay, his warmth burned her hands. The children ran as fast as they could through the icy corridors until they were outside at last.

The reindeer was waiting for

them and they raced away together, back through the forest to the safety of their village. Behind them the snow palace melted, and the evil magic of the Snow Queen was lost forever.

The Crystal Ball

In a far away land there lived a witch who had three sons. The witch thought her sons wanted to steal her magic, so she turned her eldest son into

an eagle and her middle son into
a whale. But her youngest son
managed to escape before she
could catch him.

The youngest son heard
about a princess locked away in
the Castle of the Golden Sun,
so he set off to free her. He
didn't know where the Castle of
the Golden Sun was, and as he
walked he came to a forest
where he found two giants. The

giants were arguing over a hat. They told the young boy that the hat was magical.

"It's a wishing hat. When you put it on, it will take you where you wish to go," said one of the

giants. Then they asked the boy which one of them should have the hat.

"Give me the hat," said the boy, thinking quickly. "Then when I call you, run to me. Whoever reaches me first will get the magic hat."

So the giants

gave the boy the hat. At once he put it on and wished to be at the Castle of the Golden Sun. In a puff of magic, the boy found himself there, and met the princess.

The princess told him that a wizard had locked her in the castle. So the boy asked the princess how he could break the wizard's spell and set her free. "You need to find his magic crystal ball," said the princess.

The boy left the castle, and met an angry wild bull. For hours, the boy fought the bull until eventually he killed it. A fiery bird then flew out of the bull carrying the crystal ball!

The boy had no way to reach the fiery bird, but just then an enormous eagle appeared. It was the boy's eldest brother. The eagle fought the fiery bird

and made it
drop the
crystal ball,
which fell into
the sea below.
    The boy
was afraid
that he'd
lost the ball
forever. Just then,
the other brother
(now a whale) caught the crystal

The Crystal Ball

ball with his tail and flicked it to the youngest brother.

The boy took the magic crystal ball back to the wizard who said, "You have returned my crystal ball and broken my spell. You are now King of the Castle of the Golden Sun."

The wizard freed the princess, and broke the spell put on the boy's brothers too. The princess and the youngest son fell in love and were married. They all lived happily ever after in the Castle of the Golden Sun.

Ozma and the Little Wizard

Princess Ozma lived in the faraway fairy land of Oz, in a beautiful palace with the Wizard of Oz. The wizard was a kind man with twinkling eyes.

Princess Ozma wanted to visit the people of Oz to find out whether they were happy. She asked the wizard to go with her.

So the two set off and wandered over the land of Oz for many days. At last they reached a place they'd never visited and stopped at a cottage.

"Are you happy?" Ozma asked the man in the cottage.

"We are happy, except for

three imps who are always up to mischief," the man replied.

He told the princess how the imps pulled faces, laughed at people and called them names. Ozma told the man they would punish the naughty imps.

Then Ozma and the wizard set off again and found three caves. The three imps were hiding in one of the caves, but they were so small Ozma didn't think they could cause any trouble. Then one of the imps pulled her dress and she fell over. The imps giggled loudly.

The wizard waved his magic wand, and in a

flash, the three imps were turned into three thorny bushes. Princess Ozma told the imps they would stay as thorny bushes until they were sorry for the naughty things they'd done.

But something went wrong with the wizard's spell. The thorny bushes started moving around the cave and bumped into Ozma. They tore her beautiful dress. "Quick! Change

them into something else!"
shouted the princess.

The wizard waved his magic
wand again. This time the imps
were changed into birds, but
they flew at the princess and
the wizard. One of them landed
on the princess' head and
pecked her pretty pink ear. It
gave it such a hard pull she
cried out, "These birds are
worse than the thorny bushes.

Change them, quickly!"
 The wizard was busy fighting off the birds, but he managed to open

his bag of magic and find a spell to use. This time he changed the birds into buttons.

Suddenly, the cave was quiet. The wizard put the buttons in a little box for the princess.

"I'll sew them on my coat so I can watch them carefully," said the princess. "When they are truly sorry for their naughtiness, you might be able to change them back to imps."

And the princess and the wizard travelled back to the palace with the three imps trapped as three tiny buttons.

Acknowledgements

Advocate Art

Rose Clayton The King's Magic Drum, The Three Wishes,
Moray Monkey Gets Lost, Jack and the Beanstalk, The Selfish Giant,
Trains, Planes, Boats and Trucks, The Three Dogs, Sizzle, Drizzle, Thudd and Dudd,
The Fairy Fluffikins, The Magic Fiddle

Monika Filipina The Hare and the Tortoise, Little Red Riding Hood

Claire Keay The Snow Queen

Natalia Moore Hansel and Gretel, Snow White and the Seven Dwarfs,
Off to Play Music in Bremen, Snow-White and Rose-Red,
The Hut in the Woods, The Crystal Ball

Julia Seal (cover artist) How the Rhinoceros got his Skin, Raggedy Ann and the
Kittens, Tom Thumb, Thumbelina, Dick Whittington and his Cat, The Queen Bee,
Rumplestiltskin, Rapunzel, Aladdin, Ozma and the Wizard

Laura Watson The Elephant's Child

Kay Widdowson Puss in Boots

The Bright Agency

Clare Fennell The Gingerbread Man
Maddie Frost The Elves and the Shoemaker
Sharon Harmer The Three Little Pigs
Gavin Scott The Lion and the Mouse

Plum Pudding Illustration

Monica Carretero The Ugly Duckling
Francesca Assirelli Goldilocks and the Three Bears